Mail Order F
Sharing Christmas

By
Faith Johnson

Clean and Wholesome Western Historical Romance

Table of Contents

Unsolicited Testimonials

By **Glaidene Ramsey**
★★★★★ I so enjoy reading Faith Johnson's stories. This Bride and groom met as she arrived in town. They were married and then the story begins.!!!! Enjoy

By **Voracious Reader**
★★★★★ "Great story of love and of faith. The hardships we may have to go through and how with faith, and God's help we can get through them" -

By **Glaidene's reads**
★★★★★ "Faith Johnson is a five star writer. I have read a majority of her books. I enjoyed the story and hope you will too!!!!!"

By **Kirk Statler**
★★★★★ I liked the book. A different twist because she wasn't in contract with anyone when she went. She went. God provided for her needs. God blessed her above and beyond.

By **Amazon Customer**
★★★★★ Great clean and easy reading, a lot of fun for you to know ignores words this is crazy so I'll not reviewing again. Let me tell it and go

By **Kindle Customer**
★★★★★ Wonderful story. You have such a way of showing people that opposite do attack. Both in words and action. I am glad that I found your books.

FREE GIFT

Just to say thanks for checking our works we like to gift you

<u>Our Exclusive Never Before Released Books</u>

<u>100% FREE!</u>

Please GO TO

`http://cleanromancepublishing.com/gift`

And get your FREE gift

Thanks for being such a wonderful client.

Chapter 1

The sun dipped below the horizon, casting long shadows over the small Louisiana town where Anna Larkin lived. Her footsteps echoed with a heavy heart as she trudged along the cobbled streets, the weight of yet another job rejection bearing down on her shoulders. It had become a painfully familiar feeling in recent months.

Anna had a smile that could brighten even the darkest of days, but today, her lips were pressed into a thin line. The town's worn buildings seemed to close in around her as if echoing her sense of confinement. She was a woman of resilience, but her spirit was weary from the relentless struggle she faced.

In a world where opportunities for women were scarce and often limited to a few honorable avenues, Anna's choices were few. Her father's voice echoed in her mind, reminding her that a woman's place was in the home, and her duty was to marry and raise a family—but she had always thought that she was going to do more.

Loss had been her constant companion. Anna had known more sorrow than the average person should bear. The memories of the tragic fire that had taken her entire family away from her haunted her waking hours and tormented her dreams. Despite this unimaginable loss, Anna had managed to remain optimistic.

As she walked along the dusty streets, Anna couldn't shake the memories of her recent job interviews. It didn't matter how qualified she thought she was; she was just a woman seeking work in a man's world. The rejections piled up, each one driving a stake through her fragile confidence.

Anna's financial hardships were unrelenting. She was drowning in debt, and the future looked bleak. The town's gossipmongers whispered behind her back, casting judgmental glances at a woman who dared to defy convention. But Anna refused to be defeated. She yearned for more than the prescribed roles society had assigned her, and she wouldn't let adversity crush her spirit.

That evening, as the gas lamps flickered to life, Anna returned to her rented room. It was modest, but it served as a refuge of sorts, a place where she could collect her thoughts and gather her strength. She knew she had to find a way out of this cycle of rejection and despair. Her future depended on it.

The dimly lit room felt like a sanctuary, and there, in the solitude of her small haven, Anna couldn't help but let her thoughts drift to an advertisement she had seen in the local newspaper. It was a small, modest notice that bore the name "Carl Brooks" and carried a simple message:

Wife Wanted. Must Love Kids.

Looking for a wife to help me raise my two daughters. Must be kind-hearted, responsible, and good with children.

Anna tried to push those thoughts aside, settled in, and prepared to start supper. She sighed in defeat as she surveyed the meager groceries she had left. A few potatoes, some wilted vegetables, and a can of beans—hardly enough to make a satisfying meal. It had been over a year since the tragic fire that had robbed her of everything she held dear, and she had hoped that by now, life would have taken a turn for the better. But reality had a cruel way of mocking her hopes.

Nothing had changed. The debts continued to pile up, and she still struggled to even put a simple meal before her every day. It seemed that no matter how hard she tried, she couldn't escape the cycle of hardship that had become her life.

She had once managed to secure a well-paying job as a secretary for a publishing firm. For the first time, she'd felt like things were finally looking up for her. However, her new-found hope didn't last very long. Her boss, Mr. Vaughn, was a pig and made her days at work a trial.

His advances, insidious at first, had become increasingly brazen over time. Despite being a married man, he had pursued Anna relentlessly with inappropriate propositions and comments. She knew that she had to remove herself from the situation for her safety, no matter how scarce the alternatives might be. She didn't have much, but she would not let him destroy her reputation and soil her name.

The decision to quit her job had been a painful one, for it meant surrendering the semblance of financial stability she had briefly grasped. But Anna refused to be reduced to a victim, to let a predatory man steal away her dignity and self-respect.

As she stirred the thin soup in her worn pot, Anna couldn't help but wonder if there was a way out of this seemingly endless cycle of hardship. The advertisement for a wife in Carl Brooks's household continued to tug at her thoughts like a lifeline, offering the prospect of a fresh start. She would have to travel far, but it would solve all her problems, and she loved children.

Anna's heart ached when she thought about Carl's girls. Having lost her family in a devastating fire, she knew the cruel sting of loss all too well and wouldn't wish that on anyone else; every girl needed her mother.

Unable to shake the yearning that had taken hold of her, Anna knew she had to take action. Determination surged through her as she hurriedly donned her coat and headed down the dimly lit street, making her way to the neighborhood butchery.

Bert and Sally, the owners of the butchery, had always been kind to her. They knew of her struggles and occasionally offered her free meat when they could afford to spare some. Anna had babysat their three children—Robert Jr., Simon, and Lucy—on countless occasions and never expected any payment for them. Such kindness was rare, especially in the harsh economic climate.

As Anna entered the butchery, she found Bert tending to a customer, his apron stained with the evidence of a long day's work. Sally noticed her arrival. Their eyes met, and Anna greeted her with a small but genuine smile. Their relationship had always been more than just a customer and a shopkeeper. Sally was one of the few people that Anna considered to be her friend.

"Hello, Anna, how are you?"

"I'm doing alright, you?"

"Same here. It's just been a long day. I can't wait to close up shop and finally put my feet up. Anyway, what brings you here? Do you need some meat?"

"No. Do you happen to have today's newspaper?" she asked.

Sally nodded and retrieved the newspaper from behind the counter, handing it over to Anna. Anna flipped through the pages, searching for the advertisement.

Finally, she found it, and her heart raced as she read it again. She needed to write down Mr. Brooks's address, so she asked Sally for a pen and paper.

As Anna jotted down the address, Sally's gaze never left her.

"You're leaving, aren't you?" she finally asked. She understood the depths of Anna's struggles and how hard it was to fend for yourself as a woman.

"I don't know. I might."

"You know, Anna," Sally said softly, "we're going to miss you around here."

Anna's gaze met Sally's, and she offered a grateful smile. "Sally, don't be too sad just yet. Mr. Brooks might not even choose me."

Sally's eyes glistened with emotion, but she insisted, "Well, just in case you are chosen, take some meat with you for old times' sake."

Anna's heart swelled with gratitude for Sally's kindness. With a bundle of meat in hand and the address in her pocket, Anna returned to her modest house. She sat at her weathered table, pen in hand as her meal simmered on the stove, and began to write her letter.

When she finally put the pen down and read it over, she couldn't help but wonder if it was enough. She folded the letter carefully and sealed it in an envelope, praying that her heartfelt words would be enough for Mr. Brooks.

As she placed the envelope on the table, she prayed into the silent room that everything would work out for her.

Chapter 2

In the vast expanse of Santa Fe, New Mexico, nestled amidst the rugged beauty of the Western frontier, stood Carl Brooks's ranch. He was a man of few words, a widower who had known more heartache in recent times than anyone should bear. He stood tall and weathered, his rugged appearance a testament to the years of hard work and solitude he had endured.

His ranch served as an escape from the world that had taken so much from him. The rustic wooden buildings and rolling hills depicted a simple yet fulfilling life. But behind the façade of tranquility lay a man haunted by memories.

As October unfolded its golden hues and whispered of the approaching winter, Carl Brooks found himself lost in a sea of emotions. The chill in the air was a reminder of the bitter winter that lay ahead, and he didn't know if he could endure it.

It had been nearly a year since he had said his final farewell to the love of his life, Rachel. She was kind, loving, and unbelievably beautiful, with eyes so blue, it felt like they peered into your soul. She was more than Carl thought he deserved, and he knew, once he lost her, that he'd never be so lucky again.

Rachel had been the best thing that had ever happened to him. She made living in the harsh western frontier bearable and brought color to his world. With her by his side, Carl had felt like he could do anything.

But now, she was gone, taken by pneumonia that had stolen her from him. Carl had watched helplessly as the light in Rachel's eyes had dimmed, her laughter silenced forever. Her absence had left a void in his heart that he couldn't begin to fathom how to fill.

In the months that followed her passing, Carl had retreated into a shell of his former self. His days were consumed by the relentless demands of the ranch and the needs of his two young daughters, Abigail and Mary. They were his sole reason for carrying on, the fragile threads that tethered him to the world.

But beyond his duties as a father and a farmer, Carl had no life to speak of. He had become a recluse, his isolation shielding him from the pain of a world that had lost its luster with Rachel's departure. His evenings were spent in silence, his home echoing with the ghostly memories of happier times.

He had no friends, no confidants. Carl Brooks had become a solitary figure, a man whose heart was frozen in time, unable to move forward. As the days grew shorter and winter's grip tightened, he faced the approaching season with a sense of dread, unsure of how he would endure another bitter cold without the warmth of Rachel's presence.

Life on the ranch was far from easy. The daily chores, the demands of caring for his children, and the weight of his grief had begun to take their toll on Carl. And as he drew closer to the anniversary of Rachel's death, it seemed even harder. He knew he needed help, and so he had finally placed the advertisement in the newspaper, even though the thought of sharing his life with another woman felt like a knife to his already bleeding heart.

As the day's work on the ranch came to an end, Carl trudged wearily back to his ranch house. His boots thudded against the dusty path as he approached the front porch, the silhouette of his modest home outlined against the fading twilight.

Just as he reached the porch, two bundles of energy burst through the front door. Four-year-old Marigold and Mary, who had just turned three, practically tackled their father with hugs. Carl's heart swelled at the sight of his little angels. They both had golden locks and sparkling blue eyes, just like their mother. They were spitting images of her, and it broke his heart a little every time he laid his eyes on them.

Their babysitter, Grace, followed them with a slight smile. He paid Grace and then led the girls inside. While he was grateful for her, having to pay a babysitter every day was costly. He unfortunately had no choice because he knew he wouldn't be able to take care of the girls and work on the farm at the same time.

Once inside, Carl leaned down to scoop them both into his arms. "How were my girls today?" he asked, his voice filled with love.

Abigail, the older and more talkative of the two, launched into a lively account of their day. "We played by the creek, Papa, and I caught a shiny fish with my bare hands!" Her eyes sparkled with excitement.

Still too young to speak in complete sentences, Mary chimed in with enthusiastic babbling, her tiny hands gesturing wildly to illustrate her adventures.

Carl listened attentively to their stories despite the exhaustion that weighed heavily on his shoulders. His daughters were his lifeline, the light that guided him through the darkest days.

But then, out of the blue, Abigail's innocent question pierced the air. "Papa, are we ever gonna get another mom?" Her words hung in the air, catching Carl off guard.

He paused for a moment, his heart aching at the question. Tenderly, he lowered his girls to the floor and knelt before them, looking into their eyes. "I promise, my darlings," he whispered, "we'll find someone who will love you as much as Mama did."

With that promise hanging in the air, Carl made a mental note to go into town the following day and check the post office for any responses to his ad.

***

The next day arrived, and Carl Brooks made his way to the tiny post office in town, his heart pounding with anticipation. As he approached the post office, his heart sped up in his chest. There was no telling how it would go. What if no one had answered his call?

With a sigh, he entered the post office and approached the counter. The postmaster, a weathered man with a perpetually tired expression, handed him a single letter.

Taking the letter, he made his way to a nearby bench and settled down. The envelope was addressed to him in a neat, feminine hand. It bore the name "Anna Larkin."

Carl carefully opened it and began to read the contents.

As he read Anna's words, the reality of the situation began to fully sink in. But he'd already made the offer, and the last thing he wanted to do was disappoint the young woman who'd taken the time to respond to his advertisement. Besides, he didn't really have a choice. He had been hoping he would get many responses so he'd at least have the luxury of choosing, but he'd only got the one. The reality was that he was desperate, and he couldn't afford to be too picky.

A sense of resignation overcame him. Anna Larkin was going to be his wife.

He reluctantly left the bench and headed straight to the train station. There, he purchased a ticket for Anna, sealing his fate. There was no turning back now.

Chapter 3

Days turned into a relentless blur for Anna Larkin as she continued her daily pilgrimage to the town's post office. Each morning brought a flicker of hope that today might be the day when a response from Carl Brooks would arrive, but it never did. With each passing day, her hope dimmed.

This was her last hope. The situation had grown increasingly dire. Anna still hadn't secured a job, which meant she couldn't pay her rent. Her landlady had threatened to throw her out in the streets if she didn't pay up. Where would she go then? The October nights had started getting colder as winter drew nearer. There was no way she would survive on the streets.

Anna wasn't the only anxious one. Sally had become heavily invested in the waiting game. Every day, as Anna entered the shop, Sally asked, "Have you heard back yet?"

Anna tried to put on a brave face, to pretend that the lack of response didn't bother her, but the truth was, it hurt. Marrying Carl Brooks was her lifeline.

Then, one Tuesday, much like the ones that had come before it, Anna walked into the town's post office.

"Good morning, Larry," she greeted the familiar postmaster who had become a part of her daily routine. "Got anything for me today?"

Larry had a slight smile on his face, which made Anna's heart quicken. "As a matter of fact, I do."

He retrieved a single envelope and handed it to her. Anna's hands trembled as she reached for it and carefully tore open the envelope. Her heart was pounding in her chest. When her eyes fell upon the train ticket, a rush of emotion surged through her. Tears of joy glistened in her eyes as she clutched the train ticket in her trembling fingers. It was real!

Without a second thought, Anna left the post office behind and ran, her footsteps echoing through the streets, until she reached the butchery where she knew Sally was working. She burst through the door, unable to contain her excitement.

"Sally, you won't believe it!" Anna exclaimed.

"It came?" Sally asked, hopefully.

"YES!" She ran from behind the counter and hugged her friend tightly. Though she was heartbroken to see her friend leave, Sally was so happy for her. She knew just how desperately Anna needed this chance at a new life.

In that moment, Anna's life had changed. For the first time in a long time, she thought everything would be just fine.

***

Her departure day finally came. The rhythmic clatter of the train wheels against the tracks echoed through Anna's thoughts as she journeyed from her home in Louisiana to the unknown destination of Santa Fe. She couldn't believe that this journey was real, that she was actually on her way to meet the man who would become her husband. The prospect of starting a new life with Carl Brooks was both thrilling and daunting. It was a path she had never envisioned for herself.

Anna couldn't shake the sadness that lingered in the corners of her heart. She had always dreamed of getting married, of building a happy family with her loved ones by her side. But as the train hurtled forward, she found herself on a different trajectory, under circumstances she could never have predicted.

She, however, shook off the gloom. Anna reminded herself that she was getting a new family. Soon, she would have two daughters to call her own, and she'd never have to be alone again. Her heart began to feel lighter. She put on a brave face, casting aside her doubts and fears. As the landscape outside her window changed with each passing mile, she could almost taste the possibilities that awaited her.

The train came to a gradual stop at the Santa Fe station, and Anna stepped off, her heart pounding with a mix of excitement and nervousness. According to Carl's letter, he would be waiting for her here, but amidst the bustling crowd, she momentarily felt lost and uncertain.

Then, as if a whispered prayer had been answered, Anna overheard a voice asking another passenger if her name was Anna. Her head snapped in the direction of the inquiry, and her eyes met the gaze of a rugged but kindly-looking man. Her heart leaped with anticipation.

"Carl?" Anna called out, "Carl Brooks?"

As he walked toward her, she couldn't help but notice the unique attractiveness that defined him. He wasn't conventionally handsome, but there was an undeniable magnetism in his rugged features and the weathered lines that etched his face. There was nothing soft about him; this was a man who had lived and worked every day. His dark eyes held a depth that spoke of experiences and sorrows, and they seemed to carry the weight of the world.

There was something about him, an underlying gentleness beneath the tough exterior, that drew Anna to him. It was as if she could sense the soulfulness within him, a man who had known loss and carried it with a quiet dignity.

Their eyes locked, and in that moment, Anna saw a kindred spirit, someone who'd lived through the kind of pain that she'd lived through. When he finally stopped in front of her, she was enveloped by his scent. He smelled like rich earth, and it was strangely comforting.

"Are you Anna Larkin?"

"Yes, I am," she answered breathily. Something about being in such close proximity with Carl knocked the wind out of her. Anna was puzzled. She'd never felt that way around a man and brushed it off, assuming she was just tired from her journey.

"Are you ready?"

She nodded.

Carl picked up her bags and wordlessly led her through the station, then onto the carriage that would take her to a new home.

Chapter 4

As the carriage carried them away from the Santa Fe station and toward Carl's ranch, Anna couldn't contain the whirlwind of questions that swirled within her. Nervousness had a tendency to make her chatter incessantly, and in this moment, she couldn't help herself.

"So, Carl, tell me all about Santa Fe!" Anna began, "I've heard it's a beautiful place, but I've never been here before. What's it like living in the West? Are there any sights I should see?"

Anna's questions flowed like a ceaseless river, which caught Carl off guard. He wasn't prepared to have someone so talkative in his life. With each question, he wondered if perhaps he had made a mistake in bringing Anna into their lives. He was used to being alone by now, and didn't mind the silence. He could tell right off the bat that it was going to take him a while to get accustomed to being around Miss Larkin.

"Yeah, Santa Fe's nice," he replied vaguely to her first question, his gaze drifting to the landscape passing by.

Anna picked up on his reluctance to engage in conversation and pressed on, her anxiety driving her to fill the silence. "Oh, what about the girls? How are they doing? Are they excited to have me here? Do they even know that we're meeting today? How old are they? What are their names?"

As the minutes ticked by, Anna continued her barrage of questions. Carl's responses became even more clipped, his patience waning with each inquiry. Unaware of the rift growing between them, Anna continued talking, eager to know more about the family she was joining.

Anna's unyielding cheerfulness began to grate on Carl's nerves.

"Are we almost there?" Anna finally asked, sensing Carl's growing irritation.

Carl nodded curtly, and Anna's heart sank. She knew that she'd completely ruined Carl's first impression of her. Perhaps he wanted a quiet wife, the type that was shy and didn't speak unless she was spoken to.

The carriage finally came to a stop in front of Carl's modest ranch house. As Carl stepped down from the buggy, he extended a hand to help Anna disembark, their fingers briefly brushing against each other. It was a fleeting touch, but it sent a shiver down his spine.

Carl then turned to face his two young daughters, Abigail and Mary, who'd run out of the house as soon as they heard the carriage. Abigail, the elder of the two, stood protectively in front of Mary as if guarding her from this newcomer. Their wide blue eyes watched Anna closely.

Anna's heart was racing as she approached the girls. She could feel Carl's eyes on her, watching her every move. It felt like she was taking a test she'd had no way of studying for, and it was absolutely nerve-wracking.

She took a deep breath to calm herself before finally addressing the girls, "Hello there, my name is Anna. It's so lovely to finally meet you. What are your names?"

"Abigail and she is Mary."

"My word! Your names are just as pretty as you are," Anna gushed.

Abigail's protective stance wavered as Anna's words washed over them. She still, however, looked skeptical of the newcomer. Anna knelt to their eye level, reached out to them, and added, "Your father has told all about what wonderful little girls you are. I was really looking forward to meeting you."

Abigail and Mary exchanged a quick glance, and their defenses began to crumble. Abigail took a hesitant step forward, and Mary followed suit. With cautious smiles, they accepted Anna's outstretched hand.

Carl let out a sigh of relief that he hadn't even realized he was holding. He cleared his throat to get Anna's attention.

"Let's go inside. I'll show you around the house."

He walked into the house, and to his surprise, the girls trailed behind them, eager to contribute to the impromptu house tour. They pointed out their favorite spots and even showed Anna the room that she'd share with their father once they married. Anna laughed at their obvious excitement and listened attentively.

By the end of the little house tour, it was obvious that Anna and his girls would get along swimmingly, and he felt confident about leaving them alone together as he tended to his farm.

Just before he left, Carl turned to Anna and said, "We'll head over to the courthouse in the morning to get hitched. It's best we make it official."

Anna nodded and watched as Carl walked out of the house. His shoulders drooped like he was carrying the weight of the world. She felt sorry for him and hoped that she'd be able to make life a little easier for him.

***

When the sun set that day, casting long shadows across the ranch, Carl returned from a long day of work on the farm. He was bone tired and absolutely famished. As he got closer to the house, he was stopped in his tracks by a delicious aroma that drifted through the air. His mouth watered, and his weariness was momentarily forgotten.

With eager anticipation, he followed the scent into the kitchen. There, he found Anna by the stove, her hands deftly moving as she prepared a hearty meal. Abigail and Mary stood on a stool beside her, their faces beaming with excitement as they assisted in the cooking process. Carl's heart swelled at the sight of his girls so happy and engaged.

"What smells so good in here?" he asked.

Anna turned to him with a radiant smile. "I'm preparing a pot roast," she replied, "and I picked some fresh rosemary from the garden to add some flavor."

Carl's eyes widened. Rachel loved adding rosemary to her food. She's even planted a few bushes around the compound. When dinner was finished, Anna set the table, and they all gathered around. Carl took a bite of the pot roast, and an explosion of flavors greeted his taste buds. It was delicious. He hadn't had food this good since Rachel died. Abigail and Mary echoed his sentiments, showering Anna with compliments.

At that moment, as they shared a meal together, Carl realized that apart from her talkativeness, Anna was the perfect wife. She had brought a warmth and happiness to the house he had long forgotten.

He only wondered if something so good could last…

Chapter 5

The following morning, Anna woke up at dawn. The entire house was deathly quiet as everyone else was still asleep. Anna felt too restless to sleep. It was her wedding day, after all.

She knew not to make such a fuss about it, but the little girl in her was both excited and nervous. She gently slipped out of bed and headed to the kitchen to prepare breakfast before the rest of the household woke up.

She went into the pantry to get some bacon and eggs, then set to work. Before long, the sounds of sizzling bacon and crackling eggs filled the room. The aroma of a hearty breakfast gently wafted through the house, gradually rousing the inhabitants from their slumber.

Meanwhile, Carl awoke later, feeling remarkably well-rested. Judging from the smell coming from the kitchen, Anna had been awake for some time. In fact, she was preparing breakfast. He slowly got out of bed and stretched. He'd gotten some of the best sleep he'd had in months, and he knew it probably had something to do with a fine meal and seeing the smiles on his daughters' faces as they had helped prepare it.

He found the girls seated at the table devouring their eggs, happily chatting with Anna.

"Good morning, Papa!" Abigail said the minute she laid eyes on him.

"Good morning, girls!" He kissed each of them on their forehead before turning to Anna and silently muttering his greetings. She looked even more cheerful than she had the previous day and hummed a tune as she warmed up his food. She set his breakfast before him, and he immediately dug in.

After a satisfying breakfast, it finally occurred to Carl that he and Anna needed to head to the courthouse to get married.

"Anna, how about you go and get ready while I get a babysitter for the girls before we head out?" he said.

"Where are you going, Papa?" Abigail asked.

"To town. We won't be gone for very long, though, and I expect you two to be on your best behavior while we're gone."

Anna went to the bedroom, opened her bag, and retrieved the only nice dress she owned. It was a simple sky-blue, knee-length, A-line dress with short sleeves and a slightly cinched waist that flattered her figure. She didn't own any jewelry, so she just wore some low-heeled shoes and left the room.

Carl was waiting for her on the porch, watching the kids play outside, when he heard Anna coming.

"I hope I haven't kept you waiting for very long," she said.

When Carl turned to look at her, he was stunned. She looked beautiful. The light blue color of her dress brought out the brown flecks in her eyes, and the slim skirt flattered her silhouette. He felt grossly underdressed for his own wedding.

"Carl?"

He snapped out of the trance he was in. "No, not at all. The carriage is ready. We should go."

He helped her into the carriage and, once again, felt sparks when their hands touched. What was this woman doing to him?

They got to town and made their way to the courthouse. It was a simple building, nothing like the chapel Anna had always dreamed of, but it had to do.

In the small, dimly lit courthouse, Anna and Carl stood side by side, waiting for their turn to be married. Anna's hands trembled with nervous anticipation while Carl shifted his weight from one foot to the other, clearly eager to get the ceremony over with. There were a few other couples in the room also waiting. Anna wondered what their stories were.

Finally, their names were called, and Anna and Carl walked to the front of the room. The judge, a kindly-looking elderly man, cleared his throat and began the ceremony.

"Dearly beloved, we are gathered here today to witness the union of Anna Larkin and Carl Brooks in the bonds of matrimony. Do you, Carl, take Anna to be your lawfully wedded wife, to have and to hold, for better or for worse, for richer or for poorer, in sickness and in health, as long as you both shall live?"

Carl replied, "I do."

"And do you, Anna, take Carl to be your lawfully wedded husband, to have and to hold, for better or for worse, for richer or for poorer, in sickness and in health, as long as you both shall live?"

"I do."

The judge smiled kindly, then continued, "By the power vested in me, I now pronounce you man and wife." He turned to Carl, adding, "You may kiss your bride."

Carl turned to Anna, his eyes locking onto hers, causing her heart to race. Carl was very aware that they were in a room full of strangers who were all watching them. He settled for a chaste kiss on her cheek. Scattered applause was heard from the few couples in the room.

After the formalities were completed, signing documents and receiving their marriage certificate, Anna and Carl walked out of the courtroom hand in hand. Anna's heart was still pounding, and she couldn't quite believe that she was now married.

She was now Mrs. Anna Brooks!

***

Two weeks passed quickly in the Brooks household, and as the days turned into weeks, Anna couldn't shake the persistent feeling of loneliness that clung to her marriage with Carl. She had hoped that they would grow closer with time, but Carl remained distant and closed off.

She harbored no illusions that her marriage to Carl was for anything other than convenience. It had done everything that it needed to do. Every day, she went to bed with a full stomach, and she didn't have to worry about a place to live or paying rent. She had a husband whose duty was to take care of and provide for her and his girls. However, she had hoped that she would at least develop a friendship with the man she was going to spend the rest of her life with.

He barely spoke to her, let alone acknowledge her existence. Every morning, Anna woke up and found Carl's back turned towards her, and he was always at the very edge of the bed. It was almost as though, even in his sleep, his subconscious couldn't bear the thought of any physical contact with her.

He'd have his breakfast, head out to the farm, come back in the evening, have his dinner, spend a little time with the girls, and then go to bed. The next day, he'd wake up and do it all over again. It was terribly lonely. Whenever Anna tried to engage in conversation with him, his replies were always short and curt, which frustrated her to no end.

She, however, took comfort in her relationship with Abigail and Mary. She had grown fond of them. They were so jovial and well behaved, it was impossible not to be taken with them. Anna loved every moment they spent playing with them, cooking with them, and even telling them stories about her past and her life in Louisiana. They brought so much light into the house, which Anna desperately needed.

But Anna wasn't one to give up. She knew it would take time, but she was determined to break down the walls that Carl had spent so much time putting up.

Chapter 6

As November days flew by and the crisp chill of winter began to weave its way through Santa Fe, Anna had fully settled into her role as part of the Brooks household. She'd completely fallen in love with the girls and her small life in Santa Fe. Abigail and Mary had started calling her 'Mama,' which filled her with so much joy every time she heard it. Anna had even managed to make a few friends in the community. Everyone she met had been so lovely and welcoming.

There was, however, one relationship that continued to elude her. Carl had still completely shut her out. She was starting to lose hope and even tried to convince herself that as long as she and the children she'd come to love as though they were her own were happy, she could live a full and happy life.

Anna kept herself busy with preparations for winter. She ensured that the pantry had enough provisions to last them through the winter and that the kids had enough clothes. She even got a new winter coat for Mary, who could no longer fit into her old one.

Despite how cold it was getting, Anna was extremely excited. Christmas had been her favorite time of year since she was a young lass. Her mother always decorated the house with holly and mistletoe, and her father would chop down a Christmas tree and drag it into the house, where she and her siblings would decorate it. During Christmas, her mother would prepare a huge Christmas feast and invite all the neighbors to celebrate with them. She could virtually taste her mother's roast duck and jam. After they ate, they'd sing Christmas carols and exchange small gifts.

Anna had loved every second of it and promised herself that when she got a family of her own, she'd carry on her mother's traditions. As Christmas got closer and closer, she found herself humming carols as she went about her daily tasks. She even taught the children a few of the songs she remembered from her own childhood.

Anna hoped the magic of Christmas would work its wonders on Carl. After all, who could resist the joy and warmth of the holiday season?

On the other hand, Carl was sinking deeper and deeper into his own sorrow. As the days grew colder and the anniversary of Rachel's death loomed on the horizon, Carl found himself wrestling with emotions he had long tried to bury. Having Anna as a wife was proving to be more challenging than he had anticipated, and he was bothered by how much she affected him.

Just being near Anna stirred something within him that he couldn't ignore. Her presence was like a gentle flame, warming the cold corners of his heart that had grown numb in the year since Rachel's passing. Carl felt a connection with Anna that both frightened and tempted him.

He felt guilty for feeling the way he did about Anna. He had vowed to himself that he would never love another woman the way he had loved Rachel. Their love was deep, and she meant the world to him. He couldn't bear the thought of betraying her memory.

As the anniversary of Rachel's death drew near, Carl pulled further away from Anna. No matter how determined she was to have a relationship with him, he couldn't bring himself to engage with her. He'd already had his great love, who had blessed him with two beautiful daughters just like her. To want any more than that would have been deeply selfish.

He withdrew emotionally, avoiding conversations with Anna and spending more time working on the farm. He knew it hurt her, and he hated himself for it, but he believed it was the only way to protect his heart from breaking again. So, her kept his distance, hoping that Anna would finally get the hint and leave him to his misery.

***

One evening, the family gathered around the table for dinner. Abigail had just finished telling her father that she'd baked the bread all by herself. Anna smiled because this wasn't entirely true; Abigail had only helped, but Anna let her have her moment. Carl looked just as amused and congratulated Abigail, who was beaming with pride.

Afterward, the table fell silent, and Anna finally decided to ask a question that had been weighing her mind for a while. With a smile, she turned to Carl and asked, "So, what does your family usually do to celebrate Christmas?"

Carl, who had been lost in thought, noticeably froze at the question. Anna couldn't understand why he reacted this way, but her curiosity got the best of her, and she gently prodded for an answer.

"Carl, is something wrong? I just thought it would be nice to share our Christmas traditions. My mother used to do all sorts of things for Christmas. She'd decorate the house and make it festive and make a wonderful Christmas meal that I looked forward to all year. I was thinking of doing that this year. The girls will love it!"

"Stop."

"Come on! It'll be wonderful. I think incorporating some traditions the girls' mother used to have would be really good for them."

Carl's expression darkened, and he spoke with a stern tone, "Anna, I said stop." His voice was cold, and it sent a shiver down Anna's spine. She had never seen him react like this before.

Despite his warning, Anna persisted. She needed to know what had triggered such a strong reaction, so she pushed a little further, her voice tinged with concern.

"What's wrong? Did I say something to offend you? I'm only trying to make Christmas memorable for the girls. I thought this would make you happy."

Unable to contain his frustration any longer, Carl suddenly banged his hand on the table, making the dishes rattle. He stood up abruptly, his face contorted with anger, and declared, "Enough! We will not be celebrating Christmas in this house."

Without another word, he stormed off, leaving Anna bewildered and deeply puzzled.

Chapter 7

Anna remained seated at the table after Carl had left. She was dumbfounded, and her heart was beating fast. She couldn't wrap her head around Carl having just yelled at her. She had never seen him so angry and never thought he would speak to her in that tone, especially not in front of the children. She took a deep breath, trying to steady her racing thoughts.

The sound of their bedroom door being slammed shut echoed through the house and made Mary, who was already startled, jump in her chair. Her eyes welled up with tears, and she started crying. Anna quickly moved to soothe the frightened child, cradling her in her arms and softly hushing her.

"What's wrong with Papa, Mama? Why didn't he finish his food?" Abigail asked with a confused expression on her face.

Anna hesitated, still trying to make sense of the situation herself. She whispered reassuringly to Mary, "It's alright, sweetheart. Papa's just a little upset, that's all." Then she turned her attention to Abigail.

"Your papa had a bad day, darling," Anna replied, her voice calm but firm. "But everything will be fine. Let's just finish our food, okay?"

Abigail nodded and picked up her fork. She still had a worried expression on her face, but she started eating her food nonetheless, and Mary followed her example amid her sniffling. As Anna watched them eat in silence, her shock gradually transformed into a deep-seated anger. She had come to terms with the fact that Carl would never love her, but she needed him to respect her. She'd not allowed any man to disrespect her back in Louisiana, and she wasn't going to let her own husband disrespect her either.

"Aren't you going to eat, Mama?" Abigail asked. The truth was, Anna felt so angry she'd lost her appetite.

"Of course I am." She forced each bite down her throat and maintained a calm expression as she pieced together what she would say to Carl.

Carl, meanwhile, sat in the quiet of the bedroom. He could hear the muffled sound of conversation drifting in from the kitchen and regretted losing his temper. He knew he shouldn't have snapped at Anna, but he couldn't help it.

Anna's cheerful insistence on celebrating the season had struck a nerve he hadn't expected. It marked the most difficult time of year for him. However, he couldn't shake the feeling that his anger had been misplaced and that he had overreacted. Carl knew Anna meant well and had only wanted to do something nice for Abigail and Mary. It was evident from how her face lit up when she talked about her family's traditions that Christmas meant a lot to her. He hated himself for how he'd snapped at her, especially in front of the children.

As he sat in the dimly lit room, a part of him wanted to apologize to Anna, but the other part was stubborn, holding onto the pain and the memory of Rachel as if letting go would betray her memory. So, he just sat there, unsure of what to do to fix the mess he caused.

After putting the children to bed, Anna went back to the kitchen. She was still seething and needed some time to cool before confronting Carl. When she finally felt calm enough, she made her way to their bedroom. There, she found Carl sitting on the bed, his back to the door, his head buried in his hands. He stiffened when he heard her come in but didn't make any move to talk to her.

She got ready for bed, her thoughts racing as she searched for the right words to broach the topic. She knew Carl was very aware of every movement she made. The air was tense.

When Anna was done, she approached Carl, who was seated with his shoulders slumped. In a calm and composed tone, she began, "Carl, I didn't appreciate being yelled at."

Carl, his voice heavy with remorse, admitted, "I know, Anna. I didn't mean to."

Anna was caught off guard by how defeated he sounded. There was clearly more to his outburst than met the eye. She sat beside him and gently asked, "Why did you get so upset when I started talking about Christmas?"

For a moment, Carl remained silent. "Please, Carl, I need to know," Anna pleaded.

Finally, Carl let out a heavy sigh and began to open up to Anna. "Rachel died around Christmas last year from pneumonia.

It shattered me, Anna. She loved the holidays, and I honestly can't bear celebrating it without her."

Anna was surprised that he'd opened up to her and felt so sorry for him. She placed her hand on his back. "I'm so sorry, Carl. I had no idea. I was just trying to make Christmas special for Abigail and Mary."

"You don't need to apologize, Anna. You did nothing wrong. I want the girls to have a wonderful Christmas, too. I just don't know if I can do this. It's too painful."

A comfortable silence filled the room.

"You really loved her, didn't you?" Anna said softly.

"With every fiber of my being."

"Do you miss her?"

"Every day."

"I miss my family too," Anna said, her voice barely above a whisper. Carl turned towards her. It was the first time he'd heard Anna sound so sad, and he hated it. At that moment, he'd have done anything to bring a smile back to her face.

"I lost my entire family over a year ago to a fire. The woodstove upstairs must have worn through, and my mother, father, and two brothers all died. I was saved only because my room was on the ground floor, and someone pulled me out. I was unconscious and taken to the public hospital to recover. When I returned home, I had no family and nothing but the clothes on my back. I think about them every day, and I understand how much it hurts, but I'm not sure banning Christmas is the right thing to do."

"What do you mean?" Carl asked.

"I believe that a person only truly dies when they're forgotten. When we remember our loved ones and keep with their traditions, it keeps their memory alive, so they are never truly gone," she replied.

Carl mulled over her words for a second. "I don't know…"

"We can take things slowly and find a way to honor Rachel's memory while creating new traditions. What do you say?"

Carl looked into Anna's eyes. There was such profound sadness in them; he was surprised he had never noticed it before. She was just as broken as he was, maybe more, yet she somehow managed to remain optimistic. He was in awe of her. His answer was obvious.

"Okay, let's do it."

Chapter 8

As the days passed, Anna embarked on a mission to help Carl heal and embrace the magic of Christmas. Her heart went out to him, and she finally understood why he was so opposed to the idea of Christmas. However, she was determined to get him into the holiday spirit, so she gradually made minor changes to the house.

Anna started by decorating the house with simple, homemade decorations. She taught Abigail and Mary how to make paper snowflakes just like her mother had taught her and hung them around the living room. Carl initially raised an eyebrow but didn't object.

She taught the girls some Christmas carols, and sometimes, they would put on a little show for their father after dinner. At first, Carl simply smiled at his adorable children's performances, but after a while, Anna noticed him joining in and humming along as they sang. She chose not to point it out, though, lest she scare him back into his shell.

Anna decided to take it up a notch by hanging stockings for each family member by the fireplace, including one for Carl, and surprising him with a garland made of pinecones and ribbons draped over the fireplace mantel when he returned from the farm.

Over time, these small changes began to thaw Carl's icy demeanor. Anna could tell he was still struggling with the idea of celebrating Christmas without Rachel, but she was grateful he was willing to put the needs of the children above his own pain.

As November faded away, Santa Fe was blanketed in soft, glistening snow. Despite the bitter cold, Anna was thrilled. It finally started to really feel like Christmas, and everything was falling into place. Her relationships with Abigail and Mary continued to thrive, and even Carl had started warming up to her. He no longer avoided Anna, and they were finally building the friendship she strongly desired.

However, Anna knew what she felt for him was far deeper than friendship. Anna's heart fluttered whenever Carl entered a room, and she forgot to breathe. Seeing his softer side when he interacted with his daughter warmed her heart.

Anna knew deep down she was falling for him, and she didn't even dare entertain the thought for too long. She knew his heart would always belong to another. Carl's heart was still bound to the memory of Rachel, and she could never compete.

So, each day, as her feelings for Carl grew, she buried them even deeper. She didn't even dare to hope that her unrequited love would be returned one day. That was a recipe for heartbreak.

***

With just three weeks left until Christmas, Anna sensed Carl might finally be ready to get a Christmas tree. It was typically a task reserved for a man, but Anna believed it should be a family affair. She suggested they all go together, bringing the girls along to make it a less daunting endeavor for Carl.

On a crisp winter morning, they loaded into the carriage and set off to the nearby woods. The snow-covered landscape was a picturesque sight, and the children were filled with excitement. Abigail and Mary couldn't contain their joy, and they began playing in the pristine snow, their laughter filling the air.

Anna and Carl let them play and got to work. Their fingers brushed accidentally as they inspected the evergreens, sending a shiver down Anna's spine. The warmth in Carl's eyes was undeniable, and it seemed like they were the only two people in the world for a fleeting moment.

As the search continued, they stumbled upon a magnificent pine tree, its branches adorned with snow, like nature's own Christmas decoration. The children clapped their hands in delight, and Anna shared a knowing smile with Carl.

"I think this is the one," she said, barely able to contain her excitement.

Carl moved closer to Anna. So close he could feel the warmth radiating off her body. She turned towards him with a blinding smile that always seemed to make Carl's heart skip a beat.

"It's beautiful, don't you think?"

Carl reached for Anna's face and brushed a tendril of hair away. It was as though his fingers had a mind of their own, and he yearned for the feel of her skin. His hands burned when he made contact. It was unlike anything that he had ever felt before.

"Stunning," he responded without taking his eyes off of her.

Their faces drew closer, and their breaths mingled in the frigid air. Anna's heart raced, and she felt a magnetic pull towards him. The world around them seemed to fade, leaving only the two of them in that frozen moment.

Suddenly, Carl snapped out of the trance as though he had been awakened from a dream. Guilt washed over him like a tidal wave. This was the first time he had almost kissed Anna, and it was a betrayal of Rachel's memory. He pulled away abruptly.

Clearing his throat, Carl forced a smile that didn't reach his eyes. "Alright, everybody, it's getting a bit too cold. I think it's time we head home."

The enchanting moment had been abruptly shattered, and he couldn't bear to face the depth of his own feelings. The air grew cold, not from the winter chill but from the awkward tension that now hung between them.

"What about the tree?" Anna asked.

"Leave it. We'll get it another day. Let's just go. I don't want my children to catch a cold."

Carl walked away, leaving Anna in a state of bewilderment. What had just happened?

Chapter 9

The carriage ride back home was cloaked in an uncomfortable silence and heavy with tension.

He'd almost kissed her! Anna couldn't believe it. She knew it was probably just a mistake on Carl's part, judging by the way he had acted. He couldn't get away from her fast enough, and it hurt her more than she cared to admit.

What was worse was that she knew the slip-up would erase the progress she and Carl had made. She understood his grief and was trying her best to show him grace, but she was getting so tired of the constant dance they seemed to be locked in, one step forward and ten steps back.

As they jostled along the snowy road, Anna gazed out of the window at the wintry landscape and watched as the world passed by in a blur of white. The beauty of the snow-covered and the sound of Abigail and Mary playing with each other did little to ease the exasperation that she was feeling.

She stole a glance at Carl. His eyes were fixed on the road, and his lips set in a hard line. Anna knew it wasn't fair for her to get mad at Carl, but she still couldn't help it. She hated the way that he had called Abigail and Mary *his* children. They were hers, too. She loved them like they were her own and would do anything for them, which was the only reason she was pushing Carl so hard in the first place.

She wanted to help him and get him to love the season again, but for the first time since she'd started her mission, she feared it was impossible.

The ride seemed to stretch on endlessly. Anna's heart ached with longing, not just for the man beside her but for the happiness she yearned to bring into their home.

***

Two long weeks had slipped by since the almost-kiss in the woods, and during that time, Carl had retreated further into his shell. He seldom spoke to Anna, offering only the briefest of smiles and one-word responses when necessary. Each instance of his silence and avoidance cut deeper into Anna's heart, for she had fallen deeply for him.

It was a painful cycle, and Carl's emotional distance left Anna feeling rejected and wounded. This time, it hurt even more because she'd fallen for Carl. Every time he ignored her, it felt like a knife to her heart. She'd never meant to fall in love with her husband. Anna knew their marriage was purely a marriage of convenience, knowing full well his heart would always belong to his late wife. Yet, against her best intentions, her stupid heart had betrayed her. Try as she might, she knew she couldn't resist him.

On this particular night, as Anna busied herself clearing the kitchen, her frustration reached a boiling point. She didn't even realize it when she started banging the pots and pans together as she was cleaning.

Carl, who was in the bedroom, tried to ignore it at first, but after a while, he couldn't stand it anymore. He went to the kitchen to find out what all the commotion was about.

"Anna, you're going to wake the children up."

When Anna turned to him, her face flushed with frustration, her eyes filled with unshed tears.

"What's wrong?" he asked.

Anna set down the dishes. She took a deep breath, steadying herself, and then spoke with a trembling voice. "You're not being fair."

"What?" Carl asked with a confused expression.

"I said you're not being fair. You keep shutting me out, and I don't know how much longer I can take it. I'm only trying to help. Can't you see that?"

Carl was taken aback by her words, his ordinarily stoic expression faltering.

"I... I didn't mean to hurt you," he admitted, his voice filled with regret. "I know you're just trying to help, but it's not as easy as you think, Anna. It's just... I don't want to give you false hope."

"All I'm asking is that you try."

"I know. I promise that I will. I can be better."

Anna listened to his words, her heart aching. She wanted to believe him, to believe that he cared for her in some way, but her fears held her back. She couldn't bear the thought of getting her heart broken again if he were to change his mind in a few days.

"I want that to be true," Anna confessed, her voice softening, "but I'm scared, Carl. I'm scared of hoping for something that might never be. Besides, Christmas is only a week away. It's too late now."

Carl sighed heavily, realizing the pain he had unintentionally caused Anna. He stepped closer to her, reaching out to gently cup her cheek.

"I don't want to hurt you, Anna. I just need time... time to figure things out. Please understand this."

Anna nodded, tears glistening in her eyes. She placed her hand over his and said softly, "I know. I guess we won't be celebrating Christmas this year."

She pulled his hand away from his face and went to the bedroom, her heart breaking with every step she took.

Chapter 10

Carl watched as Anna retreated into the bedroom. He couldn't shake the heavy feeling of regret that had settled over him. Her shoulders were slumped, and even the pep in her step was gone.

He sank into a chair in the dimly lit kitchen, exhaustion weighing down on him. He ran his hand across his face in frustration. He couldn't believe he had let his own unresolved emotions ruin something so precious to Anna.

His mind flashed back to Anna's bright smile and the joy she offered to his children. In just two months, she had converted his once-dark family into one of joy and laughter. Her presence had brought life to the house in ways he could never have anticipated.

And yet, all he had given her in return was a brief outburst of rage and impatience, which had broken her holiday joy.

Carl slumped forward and buried his face in his hands. He was deeply ashamed of how he had behaved. Anna had done nothing but try to bring joy into their lives, and he took out his grief on her.

The weight of his guilt was suffocating. He knew he needed to make amends. He couldn't bear seeing Anna in pain, not after everything she'd done for him and his children. He needed to get a handle on his emotions before he accidentally destroyed the best thing that had happened to him since Rachel.

With a heavy sigh, Carl pushed himself off the seat and walked to the bedroom. He opened the door slowly, careful not to make a sound. Anna was already in bed. She had curled herself into a little ball, and her breathing was slow and steady. He stood at the door for a moment, unsure of what to do. He wanted to wake her up and apologize, but he knew that wouldn't be enough.

Anna was forgiving, and he knew she'd do her best to move past it, but he also knew she deserved more. He needed to be better for her. So instead, Carl decided to do something that he hadn't done in months; he would write a letter to Rachel.

He grabbed some paper before heading back to the kitchen table. The soft flame of the lantern cast a glow over him as he took his pen in his hand. He hadn't written a letter like this in a long time, at least not since the early days after Rachel's passing. They had helped him cope then, and he figured they would help him cope now.

He took a deep breath as the words flowed freely out of him.

My Dearest Rachel,

It's been far too long since I talked to you like this. I cannot believe that it has already been a year. Time has flown by so quickly. Oh, how I miss you, my love. Life hasn't been the same since you left, and my heart yearns for you each day.

The children have grown so much. Abigail is now four years old, and Mary is three. She's growing at an alarming rate and now tries to copy everything her older sister does. They are your mirror image, my dear, with your blonde hair and bright blue eyes. They're so young, yet they carry your spirit within them, filling our home with your laughter. I wish you could see them now. You would be so proud.

I've tried my best to be the father they need, but I'll be honest, it's been a challenge. Raising children isn't easy, yet you somehow managed to make it look effortless. How did you do it? It breaks my heart that the children will grow up without you here with them.

Carl paused, his pen hovering over the paper. It was time to share the truth, to lay bare the emotions he had been trying to bury.

Rachel, I must confess something to you that I've been wrestling with for some time now. I've taken another wife. Her name is Anna Larkin. She is kind, and she cares for the children deeply. In her way, she's brought light back into our lives, just as you once did. She has an enormous capacity to love and care for your girls as if they were hers. I think you would have liked her. She is truly the best stepmother for the children.

However, as I write to you, I have fallen for Anna. I tried to deny my feelings for her, but I couldn't do it anymore. You, my darling, will always be my first love. Part of my heart eternally belongs to you. What I feel for Anna is different. I see a kindred soul in her, and she's given me hope for love for the first time since you left.

I promise you, Rachel, that my love for you will remain unchanged. You were my first love, greatest joy, and truest companion, but I owe it to myself to see where this relationship with Anna will lead for my sake and the children's sake.

All my love and eternal devotion,

Your Carl

The words lingered in the air as he reread them, the weight of their truth pressing upon him. It was all suddenly so clear to him. Rachel could never be replaced, and her memories will always retain a particular place in his heart. But he also realized he had room in his heart for Anna, a new kind of love that had evolved gradually over time.

Carl felt a sensation of catharsis flood over him after finishing the letter. He neatly folded the paper, keeping his thoughts and emotions inside. He knew he was finally ready to confront his feelings and go forward as he placed it in an envelope and addressed it to Rachel.

Chapter 11

In the next few days, Anna noticed a subtle but undeniable change in Carl. It was as if a thaw had finally come to his heart. She couldn't quite put her finger on it, but something was distinctly different about him.

The man who had once avoided her now seemed to seek her out. He smiled more often, and his eyes, once shadowed by sorrow, now held a glimmer of warmth. Carl even made an effort to engage her in conversations, and she'd caught him singing Christmas carols with the girls one crisp evening by the fireplace. His laughter filled the room as Abigail and Mary joined in, their sweet voices bringing an atmosphere of joy that had been missing for far too long.

Anna couldn't deny the joy that blossomed within her. She was thrilled to see Carl embracing the holiday spirit, particularly for the sake of his daughters. Still, a part of her remained cautious. He had disappointed her before, and she wasn't willing to let herself hope too much, lest her heart be broken again.

So, instead, Anna decided to channel her energy into something else. She spent her days doing her chores, looking after the girls, and preparing for Christmas. As the days ticked away, Anna started to make a list of everything she needed to get in town to make a wonderful Christmas dinner for her family. It wouldn't be as extravagant as the ones her mother once prepared, but she figured she could still create something magical for the girls, Carl, and herself.

She'd saved a bit of money from her house allowance and decided to include small gifts for the children, so they had something in their stockings waiting for them on Christmas morning. She was determined to make the holiday special for the girls, with or without Carl's help.

Little did she know that Carl, too, was making his preparations. While she focused on creating a memorable Christmas for everyone, he was working on mending his heart and embracing the magic of the holidays.

As the days inched closer to Christmas, Carl couldn't help but notice a growing distance between him and Anna. She was quiet and seemed reluctant to engage with him. He couldn't blame her, though. He knew he had treated her badly that day, choosing the tree.

On the morning of Christmas Eve, after everyone had taken their breakfast, Anna finally spoke directly to Carl. "I'm going to town for some shopping. I'll need to take the carriage with me. Is that alright with you?"

"Sure. I'll have one of the farm hands take you."

Carl saw this as the perfect opportunity to win back her favor. The idea had struck him during a restless night. He was going to get her a Christmas tree, and with Anna out of the house, he could easily go and hopefully get it back to the house before she came back to surprise her.

With Anna gone, he enlisted Grace to babysit the children. Carl saddled his horse and headed toward the woods. He remembered seeing the perfect Christmas tree during their recent trip together, and much to his surprise, it remained untouched and standing proudly.

He retrieved his axe from his horse and began carefully chopping down the chosen tree. It was a sturdy pine, its branches lush and green, a symbol of life and renewal. Carl couldn't help but feel a sense of hope as he worked. He knew he couldn't turn back time, but he could certainly make amends for his recent mistakes.

Carl secured the tree to his horse, the snow crackling beneath their hooves as they trudged back through the peaceful winter countryside. Every step filled him with a mix of excitement and dread. He wasn't sure if this huge gesture would be enough to bridge the widening chasm between him and Anna, but he had to try.

As he neared their house with the tree in hand, he smiled at the prospect of surprising Anna. He knew he had a lot to make up for, but he hoped the tree would be a start.

***

Anna had returned home after a tiring and cold trip to town, yearning for the warmth of their house. As she pushed open the door, she was greeted by the sight of Grace, who was looking after the girls.

"Hello, Grace. I didn't know you were coming today. Where is Carl?" she asked.

"I don't know. Mr. Brooks didn't tell me where he was going. He just asked me to watch the girls, and then he took off on his horse."

Brushing aside her curiosity, Anna focused on her tasks ahead. She lit a fire in the stove, welcoming the comforting sound of the crackling flames. Her plan was to get a head start on the cooking for their Christmas dinner.

Just as she headed into the kitchen, the door swung open. Carl entered, drenched from the snow outside, and a beautiful Christmas tree trailed behind him.

Anna's heart stopped for a brief second. She couldn't believe what she saw. Carl, the same man who wanted nothing to do with Christmas, had gone out into the cold, snowy woods to cut down a tree and bring it back to their house. Her heart couldn't take it.

"Carl, what is this?"

"How about you consider it the beginning of a long and overdue apology? I'm so sorry, Anna, for everything. You've been nothing but kind to me and the girls since the day that I married you, and I have made your life here unnecessarily difficult. Despite all that, you refused to give up on me. You refused to give up on my girls. I appreciate everything you do for us, and we'd be lost without you. I just wanted you to know that I see everything you do, and I'm eternally indebted to you for it."

"Oh Carl…"Anna said with tears in her eyes.

In that tender moment, Carl couldn't hold back his feelings any longer. He gazed into Anna's eyes, his voice quivering with sincerity. "Anna," he began, his voice filled with emotion, "you brought me back to life. I love you."

Tears fell from Anna's eyes. Her voice trembled as she responded, "I love you too, Carl."

Unable to contain his emotions any longer, Carl stepped closer, wrapping his arm around Anna's waist. He pulled her close and slowly wiped the tears from her face. He looked down at Anna's beautiful face and wondered how a man like him could get so lucky twice in his life.

Finally, he leaned down and kissed her on the lips for the first time since they got married. Anna's lips were warm and impossibly soft. He poured all his love into the kiss, and she kissed him back with just as much fever. It was everything that he dreamed it would be.

Then, someone cleared their throat behind them, causing them to break their kiss. Grace stood there, her face red as a beet, looking extremely flustered.

"I'm going to leave now, Mr. Brooks. Merry Christmas!"

With that, she ran out of the door, making Anna laugh. "We embarrassed that poor girl."

"Oh well," Carl said, taking his wife's mouth for another kiss. When they finally pulled apart, Anna's face was flushed, her lips plump, and she was out of breath.

"What do we do now?" she asked.

"How about we make some dinner, then decorate the Christmas tree with the girls after?"

Anna beamed. "I'd like that very much."

"Merry Christmas, Anna," Carl whispered.

"Merry Christmas, Mr. Brooks."

Epilogue

As the snowflakes gently fell outside the window of their cozy home in Santa Fe, Anna stood in the warm, inviting kitchen, her hands gracefully moving as she prepared the Christmas feast. A year had passed since the magical Christmas Eve when Carl had surprised her with a tree, confessing his love, and they had shared their first tender kiss as husband and wife.

Now, Anna was four months pregnant, her face radiant with a healthy pregnancy glow. She looked just as beautiful as ever. She hummed softly as she stirred a pot of simmering soup, the savory aroma filling the kitchen.

Meanwhile, their two daughters, Abigail and Mary, were engaged in a playful argument in the living room. Now that Mary was a lot more vocal, the girls seemed to get into minor disagreements all the time. Currently, their conflict centered around who would have the coveted privilege of licking the spoon used to mix the cake batter.

Their banter continued as they exchanged pleading glances with Anna, who chuckled at their antics. She loved how her girls had grown closer over the past year, and their sibling rivalry was always filled with laughter and reminded her of her spats with her own brothers.

Carl sat in an armchair in the corner of the room, observing the playful scene with an amused expression. He had learned to cherish these moments, the sound of his daughters' laughter filling the house. It had been a wonderful year for them, all thanks to the remarkable woman who had come into their lives.

Reflecting on the past year, Carl felt immense gratitude for Anna. She had breathed life back into their home and into him. Her optimism, warmth, and unwavering love had helped heal the scars he had carried since Rachel's passing. She had brought joy and laughter back into their lives, and he couldn't imagine a day without her presence.

Anna glanced over at Carl, catching his eye. They exchanged a tender smile.

As the day wore on, they gathered around the dining table, adorned with a festive holiday spread. With a gentle hand on her growing belly, Carl led the family in a heartfelt prayer of gratitude. They held hands as Carl prayed for good fortune and health. After they said their amens, Anna asked everyone what they were thankful for.

"Thank you for the food!" Mary said.

"Thank you, Mama and Papa, for this wonderful Christmas," Abigail said with heartfelt sincerity.

"I'm thankful for you, Anna. You brought the true magic of Christmas back into our lives."

Anna beamed, her heart full of love and contentment. "I'm grateful for all of you. You've given me the greatest gift of all—a family."

They began to savor the delicious meal, their laughter and love filling the air.

At that moment, as the snow continued to fall outside, they knew their love and happiness would carry them through many more Christmases together.

The End

FREE GIFT

Just to say thanks for checking our works we like to gift you

Our Exclusive Never Before Released Books

100% FREE!

Please GO TO

`http://cleanromancepublishing.com/gift`

And get your FREE gift

Thanks for being such a wonderful client.

Please Check out My Other Works

By checking out the link below

http://cleanromancepublishing.com/fjauth

Thank You

Many thanks for taking the time to buy and read through this book.

It means lots to be supported by SPECIAL readers like YOU.

Hope you enjoyed the book; please support my writing by leaving an honest review to assist other readers.

.

With Regards,

Faith Johnson

Printed in Great Britain
by Amazon

36470832R00067